Marge
and the
Secret Tunnel

Isla Fisher has worked in TV and film for 25 years. She has played many fun and different characters, but her favourite role is being a mummy to her three children. Isla has been making up bedtime stories for them every night since they were born, which is how *Marge in Charge* began.

Eglantine Ceulemans spent her childhood reading Belgian comics. She loves combining humour and sensitivity, and using different media and techniques. Eglantine currently resides in Lyon.

Marge
and the
Secret Tunnel

ISLA FISHER

Illustrated by Eglantine Ceulemans

Piccadilly
PRESS

First published in Great Britain in 2018 by
PICCADILLY PRESS
80–81 Wimpole St, London W1G 9RE
www.piccadillypress.co.uk

A CIP catalogue record for this book is available from the British Library.

ISBN: 978-1-84812-733-3
also available as an ebook

1

Text design by Tracey Cunnell
Printed and bound by Clays Ltd, St Ives Plc

Piccadilly Press is an imprint of Bonnier Publishing Fiction,
a Bonnier Publishing company
www.bonnierpublishing.com

the Button Family →

Mum →

Dad →

Jake

Me
(Jemima)

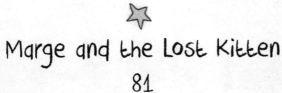
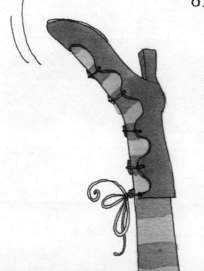
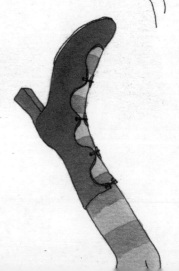

Marge and the
Secret Tunnel

It all began when I was searching for our missing Frisbee.

'CATCH!' shouted Jakey, as it sailed above my head and vanished behind the oak tree at the bottom of our garden.

Oh no! I didn't want to lose any more toys. I couldn't seem to find the skipping rope or my fairy house, and Jakeypants had been in a grump ever since his police car went missing.

I race past the rose bush, gallop around Mummy's tomato plants and begin hunting for the Frisbee.

That's when I discover the hole.

It's covered with branches, as if someone is trying to keep it a secret. It's a great big hole, wide enough to fit a bear, or a space alien, or all twenty-three of my beanbag puppies. (Although I would never take them outside, in case it dirtied up their fur.)

Our Frisbee is right next to the hole.

'Did you find it?' my brother pants, popping up beside me. He means the Frisbee, but I show him my discovery.

Jakey's eyes grow wide.

'Put your hand inside,' he dares me.

I am a bit scared to, in case there is a creature hiding there. So I drop a rock down first and it seems to go a really long way!

I gulp . . .

'This isn't just a hole. It's a tunnel!'

'A secret tunnel!' my little brother gasps.

Where does it go? Maybe it leads underneath the hedge, or to the centre of the earth . . . My heart is racing as I peer into the darkness.

'I bet it ends in Oz!' Jakey exclaims.

Daddy went to Australia once for work. He called it 'Oz' and showed us where it is on Jakey's globe and it's right on the other side of the world! So I don't think it's possible that our tunnel could go that far.

We are thinking so hard about the mystery tunnel that we get a fright when we hear Mummy's voice calling us to come inside.

'Maybe we shouldn't tell anyone about this,' I warn my little brother, who is rubbish at keeping secrets. He once told on *himself* for making a dog's lead out of Daddy's computer charger. I know *I* won't tell a soul.

Today is Mummy and Daddy's 'anniversary' – which means they have been in love for a long time. They have been kissing on the lips a lot (which is gross), so I can't wait for them to go out. It also means that our brilliant babysitter is coming to watch us this afternoon!

Have I told you about Marge?

She is not a boring, normal grown-up. She has a dancing ferret called Ferdinand and the very first time we met her she fed us chocolate soup! If anyone can help us find out where the tunnel goes, it's Marge!

DING DONG

That's the doorbell. Jakey and I gallop inside.

The first thing I see when I swing open the front door is a long, skinny pair of skis. My eyes travel up to Marge, who is wearing a pink ski-suit, goggles and a helmet!

Mummy arrives at the door and she looks surprised too. 'You've come well prepared, Marge!' she says.

'I am practising for the Queen's cross-country skiing championships!' she explains to Mummy. Did I mention our babysitter is a member of the royal family? And she's so short that she can peer into our letter box without bending down.

Mummy doesn't seem to know what to say, but Jakey has already stolen Marge's ski goggles and is throwing imaginary snowballs at me.

'I know there is no snow but it's still good exercise.' Marge gives us a hug.

'We won't be back until late,' Mummy tells Marge. 'I've left a list for you on the fridge, but the most important thing is that Jakey decides what he wants to talk to his class about when he starts school again. He needs to describe an adventure he's had over the holidays.'

'I HATE homework!' Jakey whines, taking one of Marge's skis and thrusting it at Mummy like a sword.

Daddy comes to Mummy's rescue and twirls her around, and they laugh and kiss each other again.

YUCK!

'Marge is in charge!' Daddy reminds us, grabbing the car keys, and we play the waving game until they head out the door.

Once they are gone we can get on to important business. We tell Marge all about the secret tunnel. Her eyes light up with pride.

'Well done, adventurers! When I was exploring the palace as a child, I once discovered a mysterious staircase . . .'

'Where did it lead?' I ask.

'To the dungeon toilets,' she tells us. 'But I found a pair of glass slippers and a unicorn's horn made of solid gold!'

Jakey and I look at each other in wonder.

'I think this secret tunnel leads to Australia,' Jakey says.

'Ah, Down Under . . .' Marge looks dreamy. 'That's another name for Oz, you know. I can speak fluent Australian,' she boasts.

'Don't Australians speak English?' I ask.

'They speak a type of English but it's not the Palace English. For example, they say "G'day, mate" instead of "How d'you do?" And you kids would be called "ankle biters" instead of children. Now, let's read Mummy's list. Hop to it!'

Jakey stands on Marge's skis and slides, stiff-legged, to the fridge. After getting momentarily wedged between the table and the hallway door, he makes it back with the piece of paper.

'Can we do Mummy's list after we show you the tunnel?' I beg. Nothing this amazing has happened since I rode on the Speed Demon roller coaster without a grown-up! Marge agrees, and we lead her down the garden to the oak tree.

'Oh, this is very unusual indeed . . .' Marge leans so deeply inside the tunnel that only her little legs stick out.

WOOF WOOF.

Our pug-nosed puppy Archie is barking at her feet.

'Did you dig this?' I ask, scooping him into my arms for a wet kiss.

Jakey tugs at Marge's legs. 'Come out so we can all crawl inside together!'

'Golly gosh, that would be poor manners!' Marge snorts, backing out of the tunnel. 'One doesn't visit anywhere without a formal invitation.'

She pulls a feathered pen from her handbag, turns Mummy's list over and writes:

Dear Sir/Madam/Bear/Monster/
Goblin/Large Wizard/Whoever
You Are,

We request that we may be
invited to explore your tunnel?

Yours royally,

Jemima and Jake Button and
Margery Beaureguard Victoria
Pontefois.

Marge takes a small silver stick out of her bag. It turns out to be a collapsible fishing rod with a little plastic hook at the end. Marge hooks the letter, and like three little fishermen on the end of a pier, we lower the line inside the tunnel. Then we sit and wait.

'Tell me more about Australia,' Jakey begs.

Marge pulls off her ski helmet. Out tumbles her long shiny hair of the most beautiful bright colours: red, green, yellow, orange and blue.

'I have swum with butterfly fish on the Great Barrier Reef, gone walkabout with wallabees and I once escaped a particularly amorous emu who'd fallen madly in love with me and tried to lay an egg on my head!'

Jakey and I snort with laughter.

LULU THE EMU HAVING A FLING.

Suddenly the line begins to shake and pull.
We scramble to our feet and squint down
into the hole.

'I've got a nibble!' Marge cries, as she tugs
at the rod and reels it in.

On the end of our
plastic hook is a fancy
scroll with a red ribbon
round it.

'Holy moly macaroni!' Jakey

shouts.

He tears off the ribbon and unrolls the paper.

It's a message:

Dear Stranger/Fairy/Elf/Troll/
Boy and Girl,
You are invited to explore my tunnel
I have some things that belong to you.
You're welcome to come and take them
back

A.
P.s. P.T.O.

Our missing toys must be at the end of this tunnel!

'A is for Australia!' Jakey shrieks. 'Australia has written us a letter!' I don't know how my brother believes that a country can write a letter, but I don't want to burst his bubble. (He also believes that there are little people inside traffic lights switching the red to green.)

'P.T.O.' means Please Turn Over, so I turn the letter around. On the back is a map.

My heart is thumping through my ribs! There is a house on the map, and a trail that leads down to a small stream. There is also a large X, in red pen, next to a drawing of a mermaid.

'Can we go? Can we go?' begs Jakey.

I am not sure Mummy and Daddy will be happy if we leave our garden, but I've never seen a mermaid before.

Marge says it's rude manners to refuse an invitation, and Jakey grins.

'Marge is in charge!' he trills.

Quickly we gather supplies. Water bottles, bug containers and sun cream, which Marge loads into her backpack.

It will be pitch-black inside the tunnel, but luckily Marge has a torch on her ski helmet, so she will lead the way.

The sky has grown cloudy as we get down on our hands and knees, and, one by one, slowly wriggle into the ground.

The tunnel slopes downwards and then flattens out. I can't see anything and my palms are sweating so the dirt sticks to them. I listen to the unfamiliar noises from outside – I can hear a faraway lawnmower and a strange scratching sound.

It smells funny under the ground too, like soil and animal poop. But this doesn't seem to worry Marge, who breaks into song.

'Tunnelling along like a little badger,

Digging down deep like an average-sized mole,

Burrowing underground like an extra-wide beetle.

Scooping out the soil like an undersized foal!'

'Isn't a foal a baby horse?' I ask, blinking in the dark.

'Horses don't dig,' Jakey laughs.

Marge ignores us and warbles on.

'Tunnelling along like
a slender beaver

Excavating the earth like a
round red fox,

Squirrelling beneath like a
chunky chipmunk

Drilling on down like a portly ox!'

We both know an ox is a type of cow, and Jakey gets the giggles. I can't imagine a cow fitting inside this tunnel. It's much too narrow.

I don't know how long we have been down here, but it seems like ages. Just as I am starting to worry that there might be spiders, or even worse . . . GHOSTS, the passage turns upwards.

Bright shafts of light appear around us and then we pop our heads out of the top. It's like we have been in a submarine and are coming up for air.

On top of the hill in front of us is a white house that looks just like the one on our map, and a bit like the new house next door.

There is a gate behind us and a trail that leads down to some water. The stream!

'Are we in Oz?' Jakey looks excited.

'Australia has a flat, wide desert they call the "outback" and a giant red rock called Uluru,' Marge tells him, 'so keep your eyes peeled.'

We unravel the map while Jakey tries to convince us to look for dingoes. He really believes we are Down Under! We decide to follow the trail. If we can cross the stream, it will lead us to the red X on our map, and maybe to our missing toys!

Along the way, Marge describes her favourite Australian creature to us – the platypus. It has a duck's bill and it can swim, but it also walks on land. I wish I had legs and wings and a dolphin's tail. Then I could go anywhere I wanted.

The stream is winding across our path now. Marge finds a place where it isn't too wide and tells Jakey and me to leap over.

'It's a kangaroo crossing!' she explains.

It's my turn first. I bend my knees low to the ground . . . jump . . . and . . .

WHEEE!

I land safely on the other side of the stream.

Jakeypants goes next. He runs, pumping his legs as fast as he can, then takes off, sailing into the air . . .

HOP!

He looks like a real baby roo as he bounces next to me.

Now it's Marge's turn.

I am not sure if it is because her legs are so short, or that she didn't get a proper run-up, but our babysitter looks a bit like a hippo trying to pirouette as she plops straight into the centre of the stream.

SPLASH.

Marge begins to glide around in the water.

'This is how a platypus swims,' she laughs.

Thankfully her ski suit is waterproof. Mummy is right – Marge always comes prepared!

I am still wondering who the mysterious writer of the note is. But as I look around I can't see anyone. Except for . . .

'Hey, the mermaid!' I point to a mermaid statue, just where it should be on the map.

We must be here! We have found the X.

Sure enough, next to the bronze mermaid is an old wooden toybox.

CREAK . . .

Jakey carefully opens the lid and we discover a treasure trove of missing loot! Jakey's police car, my fairy house, our

skipping rope and Archie's squeaky dog bone!

We gather our found goods and start heading back, over the stream and up the trail. The wind starts to blow the clouds away and the sun is speckling onto the path through the trees. It's time to go home and do Mummy's list!

'Look,' says Marge, pointing to a big, beautiful leaf she finds in the grass. It looks like lace. 'This is just like a snakeskin! Which reminds me, Australia has lots of venomous snakes and spiders, Jakey.'

Jakey grins and puts the leaf in his pocket. He loves to hear about dangerous animals.

We wind our way back to the tunnel, just as Archie pops his head out of the hole, yapping.

I knew it must have been our puppy that dug that hole! He is so good at burrowing. But he can't have written the note, because dogs don't know how to spell (and also he was with us when we found the letter!).

Archie takes off, bolting towards the big white house.

I chase after him. We've just found our toys – we can't lose our puppy!

As I reach the top of the hill I see a girl about the same age as me, holding a fluffy white kitten in her arms while Archie barks at her feet. That's why Archie ran off!

I wave awkwardly. I've never been good at making friends.

'I'm Angie,' says the girl.

I like her straight away. She is wearing pink plastic sandals and has a friendly smile.

'G'day mate,' Jakey says. He thinks Angie is Australian!

'I'm Jemima,' I tell her. 'Did you make that map for us?'

'Yes,' Angie says. 'Sorry I borrowed your toys without asking, I dug the tunnel and when I popped out into your garden they were sitting on the grass. We just moved in and I don't have mine unpacked yet.'

BARK!
BARK!

So I tell Angie that she can share our toys, and after she has let us have a cuddle with her kitten (whose name is Clover), we all start to play with the skipping rope. Every time it's Marge's turn, she gets tangled up and we have to start over.

'Are you a child or a grown-up?' Angie asks our babysitter, which makes me giggle.

'Everyone asks that!' I smile at Angie. It turns out she is going to be in my class when we start back at school after the holidays!

We play for a whole hour, and Archie even lets Clover chase him in circles without barking at her. I teach Angie how to do a cartwheel and she helps me do a handstand. She even cuddles Jakey when he pretends

to be a baby koala, and lets him win at wrestling when we pretend to be crocodiles. Meanwhile, Marge claims that she's a nocturnal wombat and falls asleep under a tree.

Then I realise that we haven't even read Mummy's list yet! Marge wrote our letter for the tunnel on the back of it! Thankfully Angie still has it. She reads it aloud.

1. Can the kids please find all the missing toys and put them away?

2. Take Archie out for a walk

3. Help Jakey think of an adventure to tell his classmates about.

It's six o'clock – we have to get home! We wake up Marge and we all say goodbye.

'Bye, Angie,' I say, giving my new friend a hug.

'Let's play again before school starts,' Angie says.

'Hooroo, ankle biters!' Marge says, which is Australian for goodbye.

Jakey and I try to nibble Marge's ankles as we begin crawling quickly back through the tunnel. This time Archie leads the way, flicking dirt in our faces with his wagging tail.

Inside the house we tidy away our rescued toys. Archie is already snoring in his basket, so Mummy's list is almost finished, except for Jakey's homework.

'Which adventure are you going to tell your class about, Jakeypants?' I ask my brother.

Jakey looks at me like I am bonkers. 'I am going to tell them all about my trip to Australia OF COURSE!' Oh dear, my little brother still thinks he has been Down Under! He says he is going to tell his class all about the big red rock Uluru, the dingoes and the venomous spiders. Jakey sure has changed his mind about homework, but there's one big problem!

'But, Jakey,' I interrupt him, 'we didn't see any of those things!'

'Not YET,' Jakey says. 'But we did see Marge swim like a platypus and we found the skin of a venomous snake!' He pulls the leaf from his pocket. 'Can we go back to Australia tomorrow, Marge?'

'Of course! It was only on my THIRD expedition to the dungeon toilets that I found the solid-gold loo roll.' Marge smiles.

I nearly forgot that we still have a few more days of holiday left! As we settle into the sofa I lean on Marge's shoulder and try to stay awake. I want to wait up to tell Mummy all about my new friend Angie, but my eyelids feel as heavy as Uluru. I hope Marge comes again tomorrow so that we can have another adventure – maybe Jakey will learn to play the didgeridoo!

Marge and the Great Shopping Race

'Look at it again, Jemima,' my little brother insists.

Jakeypants is talking about his new magic trick. He made it himself. It looks as if he has a matchbox with someone's cut-off finger in it, but really it's just his own finger, covered in ketchup and poking up through a hole he made in the box! He has been grossing everyone out for a week.

'No, thank you.' I shake my head. Jakey and I are huddled on the front steps at home, waiting for our babysitter to arrive and I feel like the cold has crept inside my sweater.

We are going back to school next Monday

and I overheard Mummy (who has caught a cold) telling Daddy that she doesn't feel up to taking us for haircuts and new school shoes. I'm not surprised. On our last trip to the shopping centre, a horrible hairdresser cut my fringe like a Lego person's, and Jakey kept running away from Mummy and Daddy at the shoe shop shouting, 'I AM AN AEROPLANE!'

No wonder Mummy doesn't feel well enough to take us.

But I really need a new pair of shoes for my first day back. And Jakey's hair is so long that all we've seen of him for the past few weeks is a mop of shiny locks and a mouth!

Luckily for us, this means our babysitter is coming. Marge is a tiny duchess, and the most interesting things seem to happen whenever she is around. She once taught a herd of Asian elephants to paint self-portraits – so if anyone can handle our shopping trip, it is Marge.

I am a bit nervous about getting my hair cut though. I love to play with Lego people but I don't want to look like one.

My little brother Jakeypants has two rules:

1. He will not go shopping. He says that there are too many people, and putting clothes over his head makes his hair static-y.

2. He won't sleep without Pete, his soft-toy dinosaur.

BEEP BEEP honks a car horn.

It's Marge!

I can see our babysitter now. She's dressed like a royal chauffeur in a blue satin cap and jacket. She waves at us from the front seat, and Jakey and I scamper over and climb into her nice, warm car.

'Look at this!' Jakey holds out the matchbox. Marge slides the top off and gasps in horror as she sees his finger covered in ketchup blood.

'Was it bitten off by a hungry squirrel?' she enquires, as Jakey tries not to giggle. 'Or shot off by one of the Queen's guardsmen?'

We snort with laughter.

Marge takes a closer look at the box and then Jakey wiggles his finger, which makes our babysitter jump back in fright.

'It's possessed! A zombie finger!' Marge shrieks, just as Daddy arrives and leans into the car.

'Sorry I can't come with you today. I have a business call,' he says, buckling us in.

'Mummy says that we both need new school shoes,' I tell Marge shyly.

'These are my lucky racing shoes,' Jakey

says, showing Marge his raggedy green trainers. 'I don't need new ones,' he protests. 'They will just slow me down!'

'Good luck,' Daddy calls. 'Remember, Marge is in charge!'

As we reverse out of the driveway, I spy Mummy blowing a kiss to us from her bedroom window. I really hope she feels better soon.

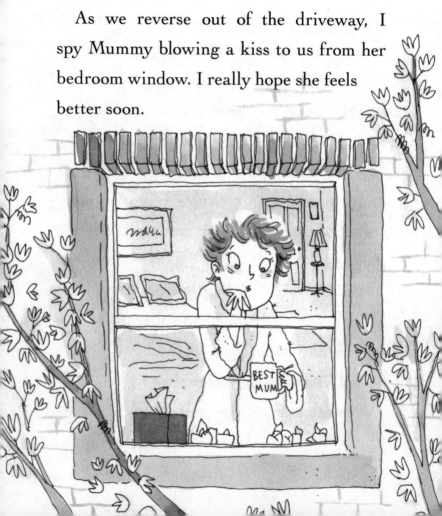

Did I tell you that Marge has to sit on a booster seat to drive? Otherwise she can't see over the steering wheel!

As we cruise along she serenades us in her warbling voice.

'Shoes, shoes, glorious shoes!
Find the right pair
and you won't get the blues.
The only hard part is
which ones to choose.
Lace them up tight and
you can't catch the flues.'

'What are the "flues"?' Jakey asks.

'The flues are when you have more than one flu at a time,' Marge says. 'Though that's still better than catching the "moos", which is when your cough sounds like a cow!'

Everything goes smoothly at first. We

even find a parking space close to the ticket machine. As we walk inside the shopping centre, Marge reads Mummy's list aloud:

1. Please make sure Jemima and Jakey get their hair cut.

2. Pick up some cold medicine for me.

3. Sensible school shoes for both kids, please – have their feet measured first.

. . . And suddenly things are not going so smoothly any more.

'I'm not going to the shops! They're boring and stupid and it takes AGES!' Jakey shouts.

I turn to see that my little brother is now lying flat on the ground.

'Excuse me,' a man with a moustache says, stepping around Jakey like he's lost luggage at the airport.

'Watch out!'

This is so embarrassing. People are hopping over and around Jake and shaking their heads crossly at us. Even though he is almost five years old, my little brother sometimes acts like such a baby.

Then Marge lies down next to him!

She grins. 'This is relaxing!'

Has our babysitter lost her mind?

The two of them are now giggling and pretending to make snow angels on the floor, while a traffic jam of strangers forms behind them. I wish I could be invisible right now.

'Let's have a race to the shoe shop?' I offer Jakey, desperately. He makes a face at me, but thankfully, after a minute, he jumps up and zooms along, zigzagging through the crowds of shoppers until he gets there!

When Marge and I finally catch up with him, he looks triumphant.

'See how fast my trainers go? That's why I am NOT getting a new pair.'

He folds his arms across his chest.

As Marge starts inspecting a shoe rack, I manage to catch the eye of a strict-looking man who is tidying boxes.

When he comes over, Marge asks him to measure my feet, Jakey's feet and her own feet too. I didn't know Marge was getting new shoes as well!

'One can never have too many shoes, Jemima,' Marge tells me. 'Kitten heels for dancing, court shoes for dining, high heels for royal visits . . . and wellington boots in every colour of course.'

I am trying to behave myself, but it's so cold standing on the metal foot-measuring-thingy!

Jakey refuses. He is busy running races. He's made a track around the mirror and keeps galloping from one sofa to the next, so we can't even get near his feet.

After Marge and I have been measured, she says we can try on *everything* in the store, even a pair of baby booties.

'The customer is always right!' she tells the salesman.

First we try on some mountain boots and

CRUNCH   CRUNCH

mountaineer up a window display – but Jakey won't join in. Next Marge and I tap-dance in sparkly purple winkle-pickers –

TAP TAPPETY TAP TAP!

but my little brother still refuses to take off his lucky racing trainers.

It's only when Marge cuddles up on a sofa in some big furry slippers and offers to tell Jakey the story of Kurt the racing camel that he even lets us get near him.

We all scrunch up together so that we can hear Marge better. Kurt was the fastest camel in the world. But it turns out he bought the wrong size shoes for his hooves. They were far too small and he came last in the Great Gobi Desert Camel Race.

'He never raced again,' Marge tells us, wiping a tear from her eye. Jakey looks very serious and agrees to have his feet measured. He says he will even try on some shoes – but only ONE pair!

I pick out loads of colourful trainers with pictures on and show them all to Marge, but she rejects every design. At last she chooses a pair of plain black ones for Jakey to try.

They look like something Grandpa Pat would wear!

I am so worried. Marge has picked the most boring shoes on the planet. Jakey will never agree to wear these to school or anywhere else, and besides, they have laces.

All this trying and choosing has taken so long that the shop is empty apart from us, and it's getting late outside. Even the shoe salesman looks exhausted.

Jakey sighs as he puts on the black trainers. Marge ties the laces and he stomps off. This is not looking good.

'Wait,' says Marge. 'You have to click your heels together first.'

So Jakey does, and suddenly he isn't walking – he's kind of skidding and wobbling . . . Now he's steady and he's sliding, rolling and gliding.

Whoa! Jake's shoes have WHEELS on them?!

'I have magic shoooooes!' Jakey hollers, half running and half skating past us with a laugh. 'I can go way faster than the fastest cheetah!'

I sigh with relief. Jake has new shoes that actually fit, look smart and don't have a hole in them! Mummy will be over the moon.

I settle on a pair of red patent leather

shoes. They are so bouncy and springy! Marge buys herself some clogs, which make a funny clacking sound as we finally make our way to Hair City.

There's no queue at all, as it's so late. But the lady who usually cuts our hair is nowhere to be seen. (I wouldn't be surprised if she was hiding. Jakey once wrestled her to the floor after she tried to comb a particularly large knot out of his hair.) Instead, there is a lady with spiky, short hair wearing a name tag that says *Lilly*.

'Sit in the chair, please,' Lilly asks Jakey.

'You look like a hedgehog!' Jakey marvels.

Marge manages to convince my brother that getting his hair chopped will make him more 'aerodynamic' and a faster runner.

He darts into Lilly's chair and even stops wriggling for a minute so she can make two neat snips. Suddenly my little brother has a nose, eyes and eyebrows again!

Jakey cries joyfully, 'I can see!'

It's my turn now and my tummy feels weird. I wish I didn't need a haircut.

'How much would you like off?' Lilly asks, brandishing her scissors at me.

I don't want short, spiky hair like hers. My bottom lip starts to wobble.

'Shall I go next?' Marge offers, seeing my face.

She whips off her hat and out cascades her incredible red, green, yellow, orange and blue hair, falling halfway down her back.

'Rainbow Rapunzel!' Lilly says, open-mouthed.

I often wonder whether Mummy and Daddy would let our babysitter look after us if they saw her crazy hair or knew that she knitted knee-high socks for her pet giraffe, Stanley.

'Can I have the top part of my hair in a beehive?' Marge asks. 'And the middle part in a bouffant, with a sideways chignon underneath?'

It takes Lilly a *long* time to do Marge's hair. She squirts some yellow cream into the ends and then massages white goop into her scalp. While we wait, Jakey and I pretend that our gowns are capes, and we have a superhero spinning competition on the chairs, until finally . . .

WOW!

Marge's hair looks incredible. It's all knotted, twisted and teased on top of her head. If we added a few decorations, she would look just like a birthday cake!

Now it's my turn. My fear gives way to excitement as I scooch back into the chair and face the mirror.

SNIP! FLICK! SWISH!

Lilly trims my hair and then does two pretty plaits on either side of my face. I look at my reflection shyly. I feel like a new person.

Mummy will be so impressed with us!

We are the last customers in Hair City, and as Marge pays for our haircuts I notice that it's completely dark outside the shop window.

Jakey needs to make a quick stop in the bathrooms before the drive home, and when we come back out all the lights in the shopping centre have been turned off!

What is going on?

'Helloooo . . . ? Anyone there?' Marge calls into the darkness.

But no one answers. All the other shoppers must have gone home. When we try the nearest door, we realise that we are locked in!

'Don't worry, my little charges,' Marge assures us. 'There must be someone still here to let us out.'

I grab our babysitter's hand as we walk down the frozen escalators. All I can hear is the clonking of Marge's new clogs echoing around us. Most of the shops in the shopping centre now have big metal shutters pulled down over their windows, and the only light comes from signs pointing to the exits.

I am beginning to feel very scared, and I can tell Jakey is too.

'There's no one here,' my brother tells Marge, his eyes looking teary.

'Exactly!' says Marge, and then she takes off, running towards some shopping trolleys just inside the entrance to the empty supermarket. 'Which means there's no one to stop us from having a quick trolley race!'

I'm not sure about this, but Jakey jumps

ZOOM

into one trolley and Marge takes the handle and grins at me.

So I grab my own trolley – I have to be honest, I have always dreamed of doing this!

'Ready, steady . . . GO!' Jakey shouts.

We tear around the shiny, empty floor, hurtling past the huge fridge-freezers and shrieking as we dart down the dark bakery aisle.

WHIZZ!!

The trolley wheels are squeaking and screeching. My legs are aching and I am getting out of breath – but I can't seem to catch up with Marge and Jakey.

I spot a shortcut between two pyramids of kitchen roll, and soar through it. My trolley is edging into the lead.

I cross the finish line in the fruit section . . . I am the winner! I think that my haircut must have made me more aerodynamic too. But I am really tired as I reach the big glass doors and I am beginning to worry that if we can't find someone to let us out, we will have to spend all night in the shopping centre!

We leave our trolleys in the supermarket and continue towards the main exit. Luckily Marge has a small torch in her handbag and she shines the way.

'Look, Camping World.' Marge points out an outdoors shop where there are several tents on display. 'If no one rescues us, we can borrow a tent and some sleeping bags from there and have a camp-out.'

I look at the rows of empty tents. It would be a good story to share on my first day back at school, but what I really want is my own bedroom with my parents next door. And Jakey can't sleep without Pete the dinosaur. Hopefully it won't come to that.

'The worst part,' I say, 'is that we didn't do everything on Mummy's list. What about the medicine to make her feel better?'

'I miss Mummy,' Jakey sniffs as he takes my hand.

But then way off, in the distance, we spot a security guard. He has just closed up the swimwear shop and is nearly at the main exit. We wave and shout but he doesn't hear us. He's so far away that even if we ran, we couldn't catch him in time.

What are we going to do?

'**SECURITY!**' my little brother hollers, skidding off in his new wheelie shoes. His legs pump back and forth as he gains speed.

The guard gets a fright as Jake bumps into the glass door just as he is setting the alarm.

'**Let us out!**' Jakey huffs, as we catch up with them both.

The guard shakes his head and doesn't move. 'You shouldn't be in here this late.'

'We had a very important "to do" list today,' Marge explains.

'And some very important trolleys to race,' my brother adds.

'I am so sorry,' I tell him politely.

We all stare at the guard hopefully, but his face is red and I am worried he is going to tell us off or call Mummy. She would be so cross if we were banned from the shopping centre.

'In the castle,' Marge explains, 'I had a royal timekeeper who used to follow me around, reminding me when I had to do things. It's a shame you don't have one of those here for every shopper.'

MARGE AND ROGER THE TIMEKEEPER !

'Look!' Jakey says, bringing out his matchbox trick. He shows the ketchup-y finger to the guard.

'**ARGH!**' the guard screams, jumping backwards. 'I faint at the sight of blood.'

He hurriedly unlocks the door and ushers us out.

'Perfect,' says Marge. 'And look – there's a late-night chemist just across the road.'

Hooray, we can get Mummy her medicine and tick everything off her list! Thank goodness for Jakey's silly trick.

The streetlights are on and it's starting to rain when we pull into our driveway.

'Adieu, shoppers. I can't come in, I'm afraid,' Marge says, as she taps her new clogs together. 'I am hosting a clog-dancing bonanza in my barn this evening. I'll be competing against Lancelot the Clydesdale horse. He has an unfair advantage, as he was born wearing clogs! Wish me luck!'

'Bye, Marge,' we say, giving her a big hug.

As she honks the horn goodbye, Daddy comes out with an umbrella to get us.

With our new shoes on, we race up the stairs to Mummy's bedroom. I have never seen Jakey as proud of himself (except when he made his sock puppet) as when he tells Mummy how he saved the day.

'And guess what?' He grins. 'I actually LIKE going shopping!'

My little brother adores his new school shoes, and I love my new hairstyle. I feel much more ready to go back to school than I did this morning.

'Are you feeling a bit better?' I ask Mummy. 'Daddy says your face looked pale.'

'I feel more colourful now you two are home,' she tells me, smiling.

We play doctors and nurses, making sure she takes the proper dose of her medicine.

Then Jakey tells Mummy that she can keep his old raggedy shoes if she wants, so she can run faster.

After that, Daddy says that Mummy needs to rest, so Jakey fetches Pete the dinosaur for her to sleep with and I tuck her into bed.

Holding hands, Jake and I tiptoe out very quietly, thanks to our new shoes, and back downstairs for supper.

Marge and the
Lost Kitten

I t's me again, Jemima Button, and it is still the holidays, but not for long!

We only have a few days left and then it's back to school.

It is NOT still the holidays for Mummy and Daddy, so our amazing babysitter Marge is coming to look after us today. Mummy has left us a list of things to do and it looks like this:

1. Jemima needs to prepare her show-and-tell

2. Finish leftover lasagne in the fridge

3. Get Jemima's school bag ready

I am so nervous about show-and-tell. I haven't even found a special thing to talk about. I've nearly finished packing my school bag, but I got distracted by Jakey building us an epic fort out of sofa cushions.

DING DONG!

My little brother and I bolt out of our fort to meet Marge. Our babysitter is wearing an orange tutu, ballet slippers and a pink scarf over her hair. She twirls into the hallway.

'Been at a dance class, Marge?' asks Mummy as she kisses us goodbye.

Marge looks surprised. 'Why would she think that?' she whispers to me, which makes me smile.

'The list is on the fridge. Have a great day!' calls Mummy from the door. 'And remember, kids, Archie is in charge!'

We all crack up laughing, because Archie is our pug-nosed puppy.

'Just kidding,' says Mummy as she closes the door.

'Marge is in charge!' chants Jake.

As Marge unravels the scarf from her head, out pours her rainbow hair. But our babysitter looks unusually serious as she shows us a piece of paper. 'I found this taped to a tree.'

It's a poster with a photo of a kitten,

and in big letters at the top it says
M-I-S-S-I-N-G.

I know that fluffy white kitty! She's my
new neighbour Angie's kitten and she's
called Clover.

'Clover is missing!' I shout at Jakeypants.
He is a slower reader than me.

'Your mum's list will have to wait for a bit,' says Marge. 'We need to stage Operation Rescue Clover immediately.'

Jakey and I crowd around the **MISSING** poster.

I can't imagine how worried Angie must be. Clover is only six weeks old! She must be so frightened, being lost outside all by herself.

Jakey must be thinking the same thing, because he says, in a very serious voice, 'We need to find her ASAP.'

I nod. ASAP is short for As Soon As Possible.

Marge explains that our first task as 'cat detectives' is to prepare our equipment. She empties out my school bag. I'm sure that Mummy won't mind as long as we put everything back, and we start to pack it with the things we might need today.

Jakey packs a magnifying glass because that is what detectives in stories have. I get binoculars, and Daddy's gardening gloves, in case we have to reach into somewhere yucky to save Clover.

'Cats love Italian food,' explains Marge as she takes the leftover lasagne out of the fridge. Do cats really like pasta? I wonder. And what are *we* going to eat for lunch?

'The most famous pizza maker in Florence was a cat named Gio del Margherita,' Marge tells us, putting the leftovers in a lunch box. 'Fellow feline friends would flock to her restaurant from all over Italy.'

I explain to Jakey that 'feline' means cat, but he is drooling at the thought of pizza and I'm not sure he hears me.

'Sadly, she retired after the birth of her kittens and got her paws on an ice-cream parlour in the Tuscan hills.'

I lick my lips. I wouldn't mind an ice cream right now . . .

It's a beautiful sunny day, but as we stride along with Archie at our side, we realise something: Clover could be anywhere in our whole neighbourhood. How are we going to find a tiny kitten?

'Let's see . . .' says Marge. 'We need to *think* like Clover. That is how great detectives work. We have to act like Clover, walk like Clover . . . We must *be* like Clover, in order to find her!'

Marge is right. If I think like a kitten it will be easier to imagine where a kitten might go. I **purr** my agreement.

Our babysitter is down on the pavement on her hands and knees. 'Meowwww,' she calls back to me. Jakey and I get down too.

MEOWWWW

We cat-walk all the way down the street, imagining our furry tails held high above us. It's fun seeing the world from down here, but Archie is looking very perplexed. We're three cats walking a dog!

'What else do cats do?' asks Jakey.

'Cats give themselves baths,' I tell him. I've seen Clover lick herself all over with her scratchy tongue.

Jakey starts licking his own arm. 'Blech,' he says. 'Tastes like sun cream!'

After scratching our claws on a tree, we cross the street to the park – making sure to take our time, because that's what cats do.

'Keep an eye out for cat tracks,' Marge says as we walk through the gates. We're all hoping to find some clues that the kitten has been here, like pawprints in the sand or cat poop.

Suddenly Marge takes off, running towards the playground. She's spotted some birds and she's chasing them, just like a real cat! Archie loves to chase things too and he tears after her, with Jakey and I close behind, meowing as we go.

We race past a little toddler.

'Meeeeoooowwww,' she says. She thinks our cat detective work is a game and she wants to join in!  So do some of her friends, and soon all the children in the playground are chasing after us. There is a huge pack of kids pretending to be cats now, and lots of very confused dogs. There's meowing and barking and irritated squawking from the pigeons. Some two-year-olds are even scratching and hissing!

Jakey and Archie take it in turns to chase each other around a tree, and Marge climbs up into its branches for a rest.

'My legs are tired,' complains Jakey after a while.

And that's when I realise something. 'If Jakey's legs are tired, then Clover would be far too small to walk all this way. So she must be lost a lot closer to home!'

I really am a great detective!

'Well done, Jemima!' congratulates Marge. 'You really have tapped into your inner kitten.'

So we decide to head home and search there. I really hope I am right. We need to find Clover soon, and I am also a little bit worried about Mummy's back-to-school list. I haven't prepared anything for my show-and-tell, and my school stuff is all over the floor at home . . .

We're back on our street, just a few houses down from Angie's, when something on the pavement catches Archie's attention. Whatever he's sniffing at, it is almost invisible. Jakey takes out his magnifying glass and we all have a look.

'A WHISKER!' cries Marge, as I carefully pick up a little white hair from the ground. It is very, very small.

'Are you sure it's a whisker?' Jakey asks. 'It could be a strand of wizard's hair.'

'Or a mouse's skipping rope!' I add.

'Let's do the whisker test,' says Marge. 'A kitten's whisker is one of the tickliest things on the planet – ticklier than a feather, ticklier than a hand-knitted jumper, ticklier even than Santa's beard. Now, whom shall we test it on?'

'Jemima.' Jakey points to me. 'She's not ticklish at all. Not on her feet, or her sides, or under her arms.'

It's true. Jakey's really easy to tickle, but Daddy says I'm 100% tickleproof.

I lift up my chin to begin the tickle test. Marge holds the tiny hair at my neck and slowly wiggles it around. At first I can't feel anything, but then I begin to feel little bubbles on the surface of my skin.

Before I can stop it, I burst into a giggle.

'It's definitely a whisker,' Jakey says solemnly. Archie yips in agreement.

Only Clover could have a whisker that tiny, so she must have come this way! We keep searching, checking the trees nearby for scratch marks.

At the next house along, Marge gets very excited by a small break in the chain-link fence.

'Aha!' she cries, waving a finger in the air.

We crouch down for a closer look. There is a minuscule tuft of white fur stuck to the fence. It looks like kitten fur!

This does seem like the sort of place a kitten would go exploring, but Marge says that we need to be sure. She gets down on all fours again and crawls towards the gap in the fence. Her head and arms squeeze through, but the rest of her is not going to fit.

Before I can warn her, Marge's belly becomes lodged in the fence, like pineapple in jelly!

'I'm stuck!' Marge sounds surprised, and her little legs are swinging this way and that.

Jakey takes hold of her feet and tries pulling our babysitter back towards us, but that doesn't work.

'Try pushing,' I suggest, but when we do she doesn't move an inch.

'This reminds me of the time I got my head trapped inside my best ballgown,' Marge tells us. 'The Queen thought I was a headless ghost, when she found me wandering the palace corridors!

NOT A BLESSING IN DISGUISE !

Luckily I was rescued by Admiral Cecil Charles, right before I was about to tumble down the palace stairwell.'

Oh no, what do we do? I wish our parents were here. Daddy would have a rescue plan. He once managed to free my finger from a doll's teacup, using only butter. And he told me all about when *he* was little and he got his head stuck in a banister! *His* mummy (my nan) wasn't very happy, because she had to call the Fire Brigade.

Wait, that's it!

'We're going to have to call the Fire Brigade,' I announce.

Jakey's eyes are nearly popping out of his head. There is nothing my four-year-old brother wants more than to meet a real-life fireman, but I can tell he's also nervous. Calling the Fire Brigade is serious. We learned about it in school, and how you should never call them out unless it's an emergency. But I don't think there's any other way to rescue our babysitter . . .

Marge agrees, and we dig through her giant bag and find her phone. I don't want to call the Queen by mistake, but Marge's arms are on the other side of the fence. What will we do?

'Don't worry, I will dial with my toes. That's how I normally make phone calls.'

Marge kicks off her ballet shoes, wiggles her toes and starts tapping away at the screen. She presses each number with a different toe.

It isn't long before we hear the screech of sirens. They get louder and louder, and soon a huge red fire truck with shiny silver wheels is racing down our street!

Out climb two firefighters, a man and a woman. They look a bit like space aliens in their big yellow suits. Their faces are streaked with dirt and the fireman shakes my hand.

'Hello,' he says. 'I'm Andrew, and this is Alice.'

I smile shyly at Alice. Jakey hides behind me as I explain what has happened.

Alice and Andrew quickly get to work. They ask Marge how she is feeling, and she requests a cup of English breakfast tea and a plate of scones.

Alice and Andrew laugh heartily.

'This isn't a restaurant – it's a rescue!' Alice tells her.

Andrew goes to the back of the truck and returns with a giant pair of scissors. He cuts into the wire around Marge's body and Alice peels the metal back. She is wearing thick gloves, so I put on Daddy's gardening gloves and help her.

'I'm free!' Marge does a little high kick, followed by a curtsy. 'I can't thank you enough,' she says to Alice and Andrew.

You are not going to believe what happened next. That's right, Alice and Andrew let us all scamper aboard the fire engine!

Jakey and I check out all the cool gadgets inside, like the emergency bell and the flashing lights on the control panel.

I think I might want to be a firefighter someday.

'I once made the mistake of sitting too close to a candle at the midsummer picnic while helping a family of squirrels steal a French baguette,' Marge tells us. She shakes her head. 'My silk bloomers were singed and I couldn't sit down for a week!'

Alice and Andrew chuckle, and then Alice tells Marge that if her knickers catch on fire again, she must remember to Stop, Drop and Roll.

While Marge rolls around on the floor to practise, Alice lets Jakey and I try on a fire suit. It turns out the fire suits are so big that we can both squeeze into one! I climb into the left leg and he climbs into the right!

Then Andrew lets us hold the hose. It's miles long and super-heavy, and when he turns the water on for a minute, Jakey and

I nearly fall over! The gushing water pulls your whole body with it. It's like trying to wrestle a giant python!

Before we go, Alice and Andrew agree to let us pretend to drive the fire engine. But just as we are about to sit down, there is a crackling voice over the radio.

'Engine Nine, we have reports of a marooned feline in your vicinity. Can you respond?'

'That means that a cat has got stuck somewhere,' Alice explains.

But I know what feline means, and I can tell that Jakey does too. It could be Clover! We nearly forgot all about her.

I tell the fire people that we are looking for a lost kitten, and they invite us to ride with them to see if the stuck kitty is Clover.

Hurray!

'Buckle up! We need to leave,' Andrew calls as Jakey, Marge and I slide into our seats.

NEEEEE-NAW!
NEEEEEEE-NAAWWW!!

The fire truck takes off, siren blaring. It's VERY loud and my head is beginning to feel rattled like a bell. I cover Archie's ears, but luckily we only have to go a little way down our street before we see some people gathered under a tall tree.

There, on the highest branch, is something small and white.

'Are you sure that's a cat?' Alice says to a woman on the pavement, as we step down from the truck. 'It's so tiny!'

Marge shrugs. 'It looks like the Duchess of Wheelbarrow's missing furry white mitten.'

'Quick!' I tell Jakey. 'The binoculars!'

He gets them out of my backpack and, sure enough, it *is* Clover up there! Angie will be so happy!

Andrew is peering up through the binoculars now.

'How will you get her down?' Jakey asks.

'Watch this,' Alice says with a smile. She heads back to the fire engine and presses a large red button.

SQUEAK ... CLUNK ...

Slowly, slowly, a ladder rises up from the back of the engine. Inch by inch, it unfolds and heads up to the sky.

Andrew climbs the
steel ladder up towards
the kitten. He has
a small cage with him.
When he gets near
Clover, he carefully leans
out to reach her.

But Clover is scared of the firefighter in his big suit and helmet. The kitten crawls backwards and then darts onto an even higher branch.

Andrew tries again and again, but Clover is too scared. I get pins and needles in my foot and my neck aches from staring upwards. Eventually Andrew gives up and climbs back down to the ground with a sigh.

Oh no – what will happen to Clover? She can't sleep up in that tree all night!

Luckily Marge has a bright idea. 'Let me go up,' she begs. 'I trained the Queen's cats – Fluffybum, Bunnykins and Waggytail – to embroider their initials on silk handkerchiefs. If I can do that, then surely I can convince one little kitten to come to safety.'

Before they can stop her, Marge kicks off her ballet shoes, grabs my rucksack and heads up the ladder. She is so brave!

Up, up and up she goes, singing to Clover in her meowing cat-voice:

'Do you like sardines,
salmon or mice?

Do you dine once a day or thrice?

Till you are safe,
Marge is not quittin',

You'll soon be home,
you fluffy white kitten!'

She is holding out the leftover lasagne, and I can't help thinking that our babysitter looks rather silly! But Clover seems to like Marge, and edges close enough for her to grab the kitten and kiss her head.

HOORAY! Jakey and I cheer and clap. Clover is safe.

Triumphantly, Marge looks down at us, and then she suddenly gasps. I don't think she realised how far up she'd got!

'Arghhh!' she screams, clutching at the sides of the ladder. 'I'm stuck, again!' Her eyes are pinched shut and her face is deathly pale. 'I'm afraid of heights!'

'Don't worry, we will rescue you both!' shouts Alice. She adjusts the ladder, then climbs up and clicks a harness onto Marge and Clover. Slowly they make their wobbly way down together.

I can't watch; my palms are sweaty and there are butterflies in my tummy. Then I hear a purring in my ear and feel four paws on my shoulder. It's Clover, and Marge is standing safely beside me!

Jakey, Marge and I all hug, and Andrew finds Jakey and me plastic fire helmets that we can keep! Then I hold Clover as she scoffs the leftover lasagne.

Alice and Andrew drive us up the street to Angie's house.

'CLOVER!' Angie cries happily when she sees her furry friend. Angie's mum is so grateful that she gives everyone ice cream.

We are just saying goodbye to our new firefighter friends when our parents arrive home. You should have seen their faces when they spotted the big fire engine outside our neighbours' house!

'Thanks again for your help, Jakey and Jemima,' shouts Alice as they drive away. 'We couldn't have done it without you. You too, Marge!'

'Kids?!' Daddy's jaw is open.

Jakey jumps into Mummy's arms, his fire hat tipping backwards.

'I held a real fire hose, and Marge got stuck in a tree!'

We tell them all about the dramatic rescue of Clover. Mummy is super-proud of us and thinks it will make a great story for show-and-tell, but I'm still worried about one thing: I haven't packed my bag ready for school. Still, at least now I have a fire helmet and a great adventure to tell my class on our first day back.

As she hugs us goodbye, Marge gives me the rucksack.

'Well done, my little cat-catchers,' she says.

And I swear our babysitter must be magical, because inside are all my books and pencils, ready for school – as well as Jake's magnifying glass, my binoculars and Clover's silver-white whisker.

Have you read Marge's other hilarious adventures?

ISLA FISHER

Marge
in
Charge

Why follow the rules when you can invent your own?

Meet Marge,

the mischievous babysitter
with rainbow hair who loves to make
a mess and bend the rules . . .

At dinnertime Chef Marge cooks up
chocolate soup and at school Marge the
Musician conducts a chaotic concert
in the playground.

Jake and Jemima have brilliant fun
with their babysitter, but will they
manage to tick off all the jobs
on Mummy's list?

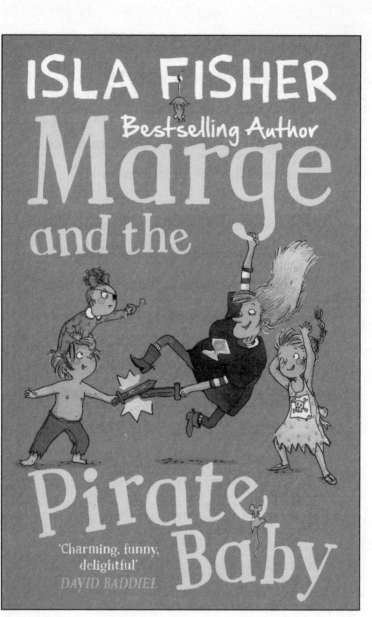

ISLA FISHER
Bestselling Author

Marge
and the

Pirate
Baby

'Charming, funny,
delightful'
DAVID BADDIEL

Yo ho ho, me hearties.

Marge is back!

This time there's a baby on the loose.

Meet Zara, the naughty little cousin who
never sleeps and loves to steal treasure.
Marge thinks Zara is a pirate,
and maybe she's right.

But will the imaginative babysitter
be on her best behaviour?
And can Jemima save the day
at her uncle's wedding?

ISLA FISHER
Bestselling Author

Marge
and the

TRAIN
STATION

Great
Train Rescue

'Charming, funny, delightful' DAVID BADDIEL

Whistles at the ready.

Marge is off ...

Things do SOMETIMES go
off the rails when Marge is around,
but Jakey and Jemima don't mind.
After all, no one else could rescue
a train, help Jakey with his wobbly tooth
or cause chaos at the zoo!

PRESS

Thank you for choosing a Piccadilly Press book.

If you would like to know more about our authors, our books or if you'd just like to know what we're up to, you can find us online.

www.piccadillypress.co.uk

You can also find us on:

We hope to see you soon!